This book belongs to:

Emma

From Mrs. B's
Little School

Dedicated to:
Miss Frickey, my first-grade teacher in Syracuse,
New York, who discovered and nurtured my love for
drawing pictures.
Herr Krauss, my art teacher in *Gymnasium*, high
school, in Stuttgart, Germany, who introduced me to
modern art when it was forbidden to be shown.
Professor Schneidler, who inspired me when I
studied graphic design under him at the *Akademie der
Bildenden Künste*, Stuttgart.

The author and publisher thank Dr. Marianne Torbert,
Director, The Leonard Gordon Institute for Human
Development Through Play, Temple University,
Philadelphia, Pennsylvania, for her comments.

Ann Beneduce, consulting editor.

From Head to Toe
Copyright © 1997 by Eric Carle
Manufactured in China. All rights reserved.
For information address HarperCollins Children's
Books, a division of HarperCollins Publishers,
195 Broadway, New York, NY 10007.
www.harperchildrens.com

Library of Congress Cataloging-in-Publication Data
Carle, Eric.
From head to toe / Eric Carle.
p.   cm.
Summary: Encourages the reader to exercise by following the movements of
various animals; presented in a question and answer format.
ISBN 0-06-023515-2. — ISBN 0-06-023516-0 (lib. bdg.)
ISBN 0-06-443596-2 (pbk.)
1. Exercise—Juvenile literature.   2. Physical fitness—Juvenile literature.
[1. Exercise.   2. Physical fitness.]   I. Title.
GV481.C38   1997   95-53141
613.7'1—dc20   CIP
                                                                 AC

14 15 16 SCP 40 39 38 37 36 35 34

❖
Visit us on the World Wide Web!
http://www.harperchildrens.com

Eric Carle
From Head
to Toe

HarperCollinsPublishers

I am a penguin
and I turn my head.
Can you do it?

I can do it!

I am a giraffe
and I bend my neck.
        Can you do it?

I can do it!

I am a buffalo
and I raise my shoulders.
Can you do it?

I can do it!

I am a monkey
and I wave my arms.
	Can you do it?

I am a seal
and I clap my hands.
          Can you do it?

I can do it!

I am a gorilla
and I thump my chest.
    Can you do it?

I can do it!

I am a cat
and I arch my back.
Can you do it?

I can do it!

I am a crocodile
and I wriggle my hips.
Can you do it?

I can do it!

I am a camel
and I bend my knees.
Can you do it?

I can do it!

I am a donkey
and I kick my legs.
        Can you do it?

I can do it!

I am an elephant
and I stomp my foot.
Can you do it?

I can do it!

I am I
and I wiggle my toe.
Can you do it?

I can do it! I can do it!